GUIDE TO THE
SUPERNATURAL
REALMS

VON JAMIE ARTLAND

Guide to the Supernatural Realms

Copyright © 2026 by Von Jamie Artland.

MILTON & HUGO L.L.C.
1001 3rd Avenue West,
Suite 430 Bradenton, FL 34205, USA

Website: *www. miltonandhugo.com*
Hotline: *1- 888-778-0033*
Email: *info@miltonandhugo.com*

Ordering Information:
Quantity sales. Special discounts are granted to corporations, associations, and other organizations. For more information on these discounts, please reach out to the publisher using the contact information provided above.

ISBN-13:   979-8-89285-742-0   [Paperback Edition]
             979-8-89285-741-3   [Digital Edition]

Rev. date: 01/05/2026

Contents

Part One
Gods and Goddesses

Part Two
Races Explained

Part Three
Worlds Explained

Part One

Gods and Goddesses

Ashthayne: Goddess to the Drow

Ashthayne is revered by the Drow and is depicted with white hair, red eyes, dark skin, and elf ears. Her upper body resembles a female Drow, while her lower body is that of a spider. She wears common Drow female attire on her upper half but remains bare on the lower half due to her spider form. Ashthayne does not wield any weapon. She provides guidance and protection to the Drow, encouraging family, stability, and the traditional Drow way of life. All Drow strive to earn her favor, with females aspiring to become like her.

Avah: Goddess of Death

Avah is the goddess who guides souls to their final resting place. She has black hair, gray eyes, and white porcelain skin, with a human female body and ears. Avah wears a black robe with a hood and wields a scythe. She can appear as either a benevolent guide or a hooded skeleton, remaining neutral to worldly matters as her role is solely to ferry the dead to the underworld or a soul's utopia.

Chaos: God of Destruction and Rebirth

Chaos possesses black hair, red eyes, and a human male body with a muscular build. His hands can transform into long, sharp claws, and his upper body is exposed while he wears black, baggy, thin pants. A neutral force, Chaos brings destruction only when the world is in dire straits, facilitating rebirth and maintaining balance. He sometimes takes a human form to investigate the world and satisfy his curiosity.

Dubree: Goddess of the Sirens

Dubree has blue hair, black eyes, and is half human woman, half fish, with web-like ears. Her upper body is bare except for seashells covering her breasts, while her lower half is that of a fish. She does not carry weapons. Dubree lures men with her captivating song, teaching Sirens songs that either lead men to their deaths or help with breeding. She assists Sirens in acquiring new songs and seduction techniques for their rituals.

Evethane: High Elf Goddess

Evethane is a high elf with long blonde hair, green eyes, elf ears, and a female body. She wears traditional high elf attire and wields a sword and shield. Devoted to the high elves, she encourages family, stability, and the high elf way of life. She even advocates for high elf females to mate with other beings to give an edge to their lineage and has taught them the traditions they uphold.

Fumbel: Undead God

Fumbel appears as a skeleton with gray vacan't eyes, no ears or skin but can hear and speak as if he possessed them. He wears a black robe with gold embroidery and a hood with gold trim, and carries a dual-ended long scythe. Fumbel is neutral but favors those unable to pass on to the underworld utopia. He helps those with unfinished business remain in the world until they achieve their goals.

Grumlin: Demon God

Grumlin is depicted with black hair, red crimson eyes, red skin, a red tail, elf-like ears that resemble human ears, and fangs. He wears a tattered black vest and pants that are frayed near the ankles, with claws but no weapons. Grumlin is evil and seeks control over the world through the demon race, encouraging them to usurp other beings by any means necessary. While good demons exist, they are rare.

Han'gul: Orc God

Han'gul has black hair, green eyes, off-color gray skin, orc ears, and two large bottom teeth typical of orcs. He wears fur trousers with a bare upper chest and uses two crude one-handed axes. Han'gul is neutral but closely associated with orcs, motivating orc females to seek strength in marriage and childbirth. Orcs honor hI'm with tests of strength to find mates or prepare for battle.

Hurol: God of Lintherals

Hurol is characterized by white hair, brown eyes, brown skin, and human-like ears. He resembles a typical human male but has two long claws between his fingers. He wears a silk brown robe, exposing only his hands and feet. Hurol is good and supports the Lintherals, teaching them family values and traditions. Worshipped in Talania, he was brought to the main world through DNA extracted from meteorites.

Huros: Human Divine God

Huros has long blonde hair, with one green eye and one blue eye, and a muscular human male body. He wears clean white robes and uses light magic instead of weapons. Huros is good and divine, often confused with his evil twin brother Lynth. He stands for humanity, encouraging kindness to all races and peace through interbreeding with other beings.

Jubilee: Goddess of the Amazonians

Jubilee is a muscular woman with red hair, green eyes, tanned skin, and human features. She is dressed in golden female battle armor and equipped with a long sword and large round shield. Affectionate towards Amazonian women, Jubilee promotes the birth of strong women to continue their traditions and has taught them self-defense and the art of war.

Kil'iah: Goddess of the Blood Elves

Kil'iah has red hair, red crimson eyes, tanned skin, elf ears, and an elven female body. She wears a red long V-shaped dress and carries dual daggers. As a vampire elf goddess, Kil'iah is closely tied to blood elves, who cannot reproduce and must turn others to their cause. She instructed the first blood elves on how to convert others.

Kir'in: God of the Wood Elves

Kir'in features long brown hair, brown eyes, elf ears, and a slender yet muscular body. He is dressed in furs and wields a bow. Kir'in is good, upholding wood elf traditions and celebrations, and encourages mating with other beings for strength. He teaches wood elves archery, survival, hunting, and how to live harmoniously in the forest.

Litharia: Goblin Goddess

Litharia has green hair, green eyes, green skin, goblin ears, and a female body. She wears brown leather clothing and is armed with a dagger and crossbow. Mischievous yet kind, Litharia is humble toward the goblin race, allowing female goblins to mate with other beings. She taught goblins family values, tradition, and thrives on mischief—except among goblins.

Lymis: Dwarf God

Lymis is depicted with short brown hair, brown eyes, a long brown beard, and a muscular body taller than the typical dwarf. He wears golden heavy battle armor and carries a short sword and large kite shield. Known as a drunken god, Lymis taught dwarves blacksmithing, liquor, and mining. He encourages alliances and mating with other beings, with dwarves seeking his favor through their crafts.

Lynth: Human Evil God

Lynth has long blonde hair, with one green eye and one blue eye, and a muscular human male body. He wears clean white robes and uses light magic instead of weapons. Unlike his twin brother Huros, Lynth is evil and malicious, encouraging humanity to commit evil acts and promoting chaos through violence.

Nyx: Vampire Goddess

Nyx has long white hair, red crimson eyes, pale humanlike skin, and a female body. She wears a gothic-style dress, relying on her long nails and fangs as weapons. Often misunderstood as evil, Nyx cares deeply for the vampire race, allowing them to mate with other races. She is often confused with Kil'iah, the blood elf goddess.

Phyrio: Gnome God

Phyrio is taller than a typical gnome, with short dirty blonde hair, blue eyes, and a skinny, muscular build. He wears leather clothing and utilizes technology-based weapons. Phyrio is fond of gnomes, encouraging invention and renovation through science and technology, and permits mating with other beings.

Selene: Goddess of Lycanthropes and Werewolves

Selene has black hair, black eyes without irises, and a human-like female body. She wears a dress that glistens like starlight. Selene cares for lycanthropes and werewolves, using the wolf's bond to determine mates, which can extend lifespans if bonded with longer-lived beings.

Soriah: Goddess of the Talons

Soriah has long blonde hair, blue eyes, a human-like female body, and long black angel wings. She wears angelic heavy armor and carries a spear and shield. Soriah favors the Talons, an angelic humanoid race on Talania, and is considered good, though her teachings are sometimes misinterpreted by her followers. She allows her followers to mate with other beings.

Witharia: Goddess of the Mountain Elves

Witharia has long white hair, green eyes, tan skin, elf ears, and a female body. She wears traditional mountain elf clothing and wields a two-handed elven sword. Revered by mountain elves, Witharia taught them to thrive in the mountains, craft, mine, and survive in cold climates. She allows followers to mate with other beings.

Zypherion: Dragon God

Zypherion appears in dragon form as a large silver dragon with silver eyes and black horns, or in human vestige with long white hair and a muscular build. As a human, he wears royal blue and gold attire and has no weapons. Zypherion values wisdom and balance among beings, treating all with respect. He permits followers to mate with other beings, allowing dragon kin to share their heart with mortal mates.

Gods and Goddesses Name Pronunciation

- Ashthayne (ash-thane)
- Avah (a-vaa)
- Chaos (kay-ass)
- Dubree (due-bree)
- Evethane (eve-thane)
- Fumbel (fume-el)
- Grumlin (grum-lin)
- Han'gul (han-guul)
- Hurol (her-ol)
- Huros (her-oss)
- Jubilee (joo-buh-lee)
- Kil'iah (kill-e-ah)
- Kir'in (keer-in)
- Litharia (lith-area)
- Lymis (lee-miss)
- Lynth (lin-th)
- Nyx (nix)
- Phyrio (fye-rio)
- Selene (suh-leen)
- Soriah (soar-e-ah)
- Witharia (with-area)
- Zypherion (zeph-er-ee-on)

Part Two

Races Explained

Amazonians

The Amazonian race consists primarily of women who excel in combat. Their armor and weapons vary depending on the protection needed, ranging from swords, shields, spears, bows, axes, to two-handed weaponry. Armor types include light, medium, and some heavy plate, all designed for maneuverability. Amazonian women typically stand between 6' and 7'6". They are muscular and sometimes kidnap males for reproduction; females are allowed to join, but male children are not permitted. Amazonians keep to themselves and fiercely defend their territory.

Blood Elves

Blood elves are vampire elves who sustain themselves by drinking the blood of their enemies. Their armor is typically cloth or leather, allowing for agility and stealth. Weapons include polearms, bows, short swords, daggers, magical staves, and quarter staves. Males are generally 5' to 6' tall, while females are 4' to 5'. Unable to reproduce naturally, blood elves must turn other elves to increase their numbers. They gain power from the blood they consume and, while usually keeping to themselves, can be destructive if provoked.

Demons

Demons are usually evil, but some good individuals exist. They typically do not use weapons, and their armor is ordinary clothing. Male demons range from 6' to 7', and females from 5' to 6'. Demons can reproduce with other beings, resulting in half-breeds, and gain power by devouring souls. While their allegiance leans towards evil and destruction, a few desire peace and coexistence.

Dragons

Dragons may be beastly or wise, capable of interacting with other species. Royal dragons are more sophisticated, while lesser dragons are more bestial. High dragons can shift between dragon form and human vestige and are immortal. Dragon scales are harder than steel, except for obsidian metal. High dragons wear fine clothing and wield weapons made of precious metals. Male dragons reach 10' to 11' in dragon form and 9' to 10' as humans; females are 9' to 10' in dragon form and 8' to 9' as humans. Dragons lay eggs, mate with other species to create hybrids, and can be good, evil, or simply hunt for survival.

Drows

Drows are dark elves who live in the undercroft, possessing varied skills that contribute to a stable community. They are immortal. Drow armor and weapons depend on class: warriors and paladins wear heavy armor with sword and shield; rogues use leather armor and one-handed swords or daggers; mages and healers wear cloth and use staves. Males stand 5'9" to 5'11"; females, 5'6" to 5'9". Drows can breed with other races and are often discriminated against. Their allegiances vary depending on doctrine and association with other realms.

Dwarves

Dwarves are short, stocky humanoids known for their craftsmanship, particularly in metal and ore. Warriors and paladins wear heavy armor, hunters and rogues use light to medium armor, and spellcasters and blacksmiths wear cloth. Weapons are self-crafted. Males are 4'11" to 5'1" tall and have thick beards; females are 4'6" to 4'11". Dwarves can breed with other races and are both excellent blacksmiths and miners. Their allegiances can be good or evil, but they usually associate with other humanoids except Drows due to misunderstandings.

Gnomes

Gnomes are shorter than dwarves and often mistaken for children. They are renowned for tinkering and engineering. Armor ranges from heavy for warriors, to light and medium for rogues, and cloth for healers and mages. Male gnomes are 3'11" to 4'3"; females, 3'1" to 3'11". They can breed with other beings and are highly intelligent, especially in crafting technology. Their allegiances depend on surrounding humanoids, and they avoid Drows due to misunderstandings.

Goblins

Goblins are similar in size to gnomes, with long pointed ears and green or brown skin. Warriors wear heavy armor, rogues use light to medium armor, and mages use light armor. Males stand 3'11" to 4'3"; females, 3'1" to 3'11". Goblins can breed with other beings and typically keep to themselves due to misunderstandings. They can be cutthroat, especially regarding money, and their allegiances depend on their surroundings.

Humans

Humans are the standard humanoid race, with diverse languages, cultures, and religions. Weapons and armor vary with the age, era, and environment. Males are 5'1" to 6'5"; females, 5' to 6'4". Humans can mate with other beings, and their allegiances are highly individual, with an understanding of dwarves and gnomes.

High Elves

High elves are a taller version of elves and almost the same height as the tallest humans. Weapons and armor are that of heavy armor, medium armor, and light armor depending on their class, also immortal. Males are typically 5'1" to 6'4"; and females are 5' to 6'3". The high elves can mate with other species. Their allegiances can be good or evil depending on those surrounding them.

Lintherals

Lintherals are a race of beings on the planet of Talania, a humanoid type being with two distinctive long claws between the pointer finger and middle finger and the other between the third finger and the pinky finger on both hands. Weapons and armor they only wear clothes, and they can use their claws as weapons due to the strength and durability of their bone like claws that can be used for mining. Males typically are 6' to 7' tall; females are 5' to 6' tall. They can breed with other beings, though due to a tragedy of their world nothing is known of the subspecies it would generate. Their allegiances can be good or evil depending upon their situation.

Lycanthropes

Lycanthropes are humans that can transform into giant wolves that if permitted can be ridden like horses. Lycanthropes are very intelligent unlike werewolves in their transformed state can not communicate while in their wolf state except through mind link. They stand on four paws instead of on two legs like werewolves. Lycanthropes can transform at will and retain their sense of self. The alpha wolves are much larger than the rest of the pack of lycanthrope counter parts weakness is silver. Their weapons and armor are just leather armor while they can carry weapons if they choose to be able to fight in small spaces where transformations are not feasible but masters of hand-to-hand combat. They can breed with other beings if their inner wolf chooses the mate and takes on the life span of their mate. Males usually stand 6' to 6'6" (human form) between 6'6" and 7' tall (wolf form) and 7'5" for alpha wolves; and females stand 5'6" to 6' tall (human form) and 5'8" and 6'6" (wolf form) and 7' for (alpha wolf for female). Their allegiances can be good or evil depending on the individual and pack.

Mountain Elves

Mountain elves are like the Drow but reside in the mountains and everything about them is similar except they are not under a misunderstanding to the Drow. They are immortal. Mountain elven armor and weapons depend on class: warriors and paladins wear heavy armor with sword and shield; rogues use leather armor and one-handed swords or daggers; mages and healers wear cloth and use staves. Males stand 5'9" to 5'11"; females, 5'6" to 5'9". Mountain elves can breed with other races and are often discriminated against. Their allegiances vary depending on doctrine and association with other realms.

Orcs

Orcs are a battle-hardened race mostly comprised of warriors and shamans. Orcs value strength over everything else and do not submit unless defeated in battle. Weapons and armor are made of ore and generally either heavy or leather types. They are typically more muscular than other beings. Their skin color varies between green and grey. Males stand between 6' and 7' tall while females stand between 6' and 7' tall. They can mate with other beings. Their allegiances can be good or evil depending on the beings surrounding them.

Sirens

Sirens are creatures of the deep waters often mistaken for mermaids but can be more manipulating than other beings. Sirens can take human form while on land and a merfolk while in the water and can breathe underwater. Mostly women are sirens. They find men to repopulate their species and generally give birth to girls the boys are usually sent to other realms to be raised by other beings. Weapons and armor are usually nothing in their merfolk form in the water due to restrictions underwater and on land they wear normal clothes. Their song can lure those who fall prey to the depths, and they will use their fangs to drain the life force of their mates. Females stand typically 5' to 6' tall in human form and they are about 6' to 7' long in their merfolk form. Will typically breed with males for offspring their merfolk form is that of a woman and the bottom half a long fin to help them navigate the waters. Siren's allegiances are mischievous neither good nor evil they just look for males to reproduce.

Talons

Talons are a being also from Talania just like the Lintherals, but their appearance is completely different because they look like angels with large black wings sprouting out of their shoulder blades. They can fly at abnormal speeds and at high altitudes. Weapons and armor are varied depending on the jobs and needs of the people and rule over the Lintherals with an iron fist. Males stand between 6' and 6'9" and females stand between 6' and 6'5". They can mate with other beings but same with Lintherals, the hybrids are unknown. They can be good or evil depending upon the individual.

Undead

Undead is a combination of all species or beings. Most can be skeletons some can be ghouls or death knights. There is a wide range of undead, even zombies can be classified with the undead which they possess no intelligence except for a rare few that are able to retain their thoughts and memories of their life before undeath. Their height varies depending on their race or being before their undeath. They can mate with other species but cannot reproduce. Undead are neither good nor evil due to low to no intelligence unless they remember their life before their undeath which they will retain their previous allegiances.

Vampires

Vampires are one case of intelligence of the undead because they are turned if the master wishes it. Vampires can walk out in the sunlight along with other beings and they look no different than that of other living beings except all beings except for sirens are captivated by their appearance. They are like sirens, but sirens can't be captivated by vampires' looks or voice and the same can be said about the vampires can't be captivated by a siren. Vampires can be any race, and their height depends upon the original race they were before their transformation. Weapons and armor the vampires typically wear clothes due to their impervious bodies except for a weakness to silver and also have abilities. Their weapons they can use any weapons they want as well as their claws and fangs. They can mate with other beings there is a small possibility of offspring is a male vampire has a mortal woman, but they end up creating other vampires but having their victI'm drink their blood of a vampire. Vampires are neither good nor evil, but they can be either depending on the individual.

Werewolves

Werewolves share the same beast blood of the wolf. Though the transformation is not the same. They can only transform during a full moon, and they are not able to tell friend from foe during their transformed state. They can only bite or scratch a victI'm in order to create another werewolf. Those that are born of a werewolf end up becoming a lycanthrope. When in their beast form, they look like a humanoid wolf standing on two legs and their hands look like long claws their face looks like a wolf along with wolf ears and tail. Weapons and armor they don't have weapons or armor while in their transformed state they use their fangs and claws. When not in their transformed state they can wear weapons and armor of their race. They can mate with other races but only create other werewolves by a bite or a scratch, also weak against silver. Werewolves are immortal. They can be good or evil in their normal state but in their transformed state they lose all sense of self except other werewolves.

Wood Elves

Wood elves are a race of elves similar to that of the mountain elves, but they live in the woods and forests. They are primarily hunters and farmers as well as woodcrafters. Weapons and armor they wear traditional wood elf attire which is like silk robes or tunics and weapons they use are from ore that they mine or gather they primarily use bows swords and daggers efficient for hunting and fishing. Males stand 5'9" to 5'11"; females, 5'6" to 5'9". Wood elves are immortal and can breed with other races. Wood elves can be good or evil depending on the individual or circumstances.

Part Three

Worlds Explained

Etherium:

Is the after life of majority of the dead if they are lucky to wind up here. When those who die will meet with their Deity. Then be placed either in paradise of their god or goddess; or sent to a damnation of their god or goddess. Which all races will meet Avah before setting forth to their final eternity. Drows go to Gor'tir for their paradise and Mor'tir for damnation. Sirens go to Palon for paradise and Valon for damnation. High elves go to Tor'zem for paradise and Yor'zem for damnation. Undead go to the being that they were in life before undeath. Demons go to Pirin for a better damnation and Dririn for worse damnation. Orcs go to Mort'ain for paradise and Gor'tain for damnation. Lintherals go to Notoram for paradise and Hotoram for damnation. Humans go to Turor for paradise and Rotra for damnation. Amazons go to Yugway for paradise and Vugway for damnation. Blood elves go to Ug'rol for paradise and Tug'ral for damnation. Wood elves go to Jo'tel for paradise and Ir'tel for damnation. Goblins go to Goldreen for paradise and Brassol for damnation. Dwarves got to Honwol for paradise and Nonwol for damnation. Vampires go to the after life of their soul before turning usually to damnation of their being. Gnomes go to Gorwan for paradise and Torwan for damnation. Lycanthropes and Werewolves can choose Blitheria with the goddess Selene or go to the race of their being besides a werewolf or lycanthrope.

Talons go to Talonia for paradise and Rolonia for damnation. Mountain elves go to Moc'tor for paradise and Roc'tor for damnation. Dragons go to the stars for paradise and disappear for damnation. Each beings after life is catered to their lives and the way they lived whether good or evil. Upon arrival they meet Avah, and she guides them to their destination.

Mirin:

The size of the planet is eleven times bigger than Earth, the same size as Jupiter. With breathable air and lands and water that is able to drink. In this world there are multiple continents and various races and beings. At some point most of the races and beings have been at war and strife. There is magic and other sources of abilities sprouting among the beings. The only two races that were not on the planet in the beginning were the Talons and Lintherals. Setting in the beginning is that of the Middle Ages time period on Earth. And time will progress almost similarly to Earth. At the time all the races have their own regions and ways of government which is typically a monarchy. There are three moons their names are Tirin, Murinah, and Annorith. There is the same gravity as Earth, and the moons have the same gravity as the moon for Earth.

Talania:

The size of this world is that of Mars which is almost half the size of Earth. Which has breathable air and water and only has two races, the Talons and the Lintherals. There is only one large continent to where the two races reside in. The Gravity is twice that of Mirin. The Talons rule over the Lintherals with an iron fist and is around at the same time as Mirin before is destruction due to the rapid decline in resources and the planets collapse due to war.